Becky

To the
children of Cairo,
Illinois. I hope
you enjoy the book.
Karen Hirsch, author
9-13-98

Becky

by Karen Hirsch

pictures by Jo Esco

CAROLRHODA BOOKS

MINNEAPOLIS, MINNESOTA USA

LIBRARY OF CONGRESS CATALOGING IN PUBLICATION DATA

Hirsch, Karen.
Becky.

Summary: A deaf child lives with a hearing family while
she attends school and enables them to become conscious
of problems facing the deaf.

[1. Deaf—Fiction. 2. Friendship—Fiction. 3. Physically
handicapped—Fiction] I. Esco, Jo. II. Title.

PZ7.H59788Be   [E]   80-27619
ISBN 0-87614-144-0   AACR2

1 2 3 4 5 6 7 8 9 10 86 85 84 83 82 81

120815

Becky

Becky can't hear. When she was a baby she had a sickness that made her deaf. Even with her hearing aid, Becky can hear only big, loud noises. She can't hear our voices at all.

Becky is my part-time sister. She lives with our family from Monday until Friday so she can go to school. She has a real mom and dad and brothers and sisters, and she lives with them when it's not schooltime. They live on a farm.

It was a long time ago when I found out that Becky was coming to stay with us. I didn't like it.

"Why does she have to stay here, Mom?" I asked. "I don't want a kid here who I don't even know."

"I read a newspaper article about the hearing impaired program," my mom answered. "It said that homes were needed for the out-of-town children, and we have an extra room." She gave me a little hug. "Don't worry. You'll get to know her."

I wasn't so sure. That extra room had been my brother's and my playroom. Now they made it into a bedroom for Becky. Neither of us liked that. And how could I get to know her? She was deaf.

I was surprised when I first saw Becky. That was two years ago. I guess I thought she'd look different from other people. But there she was, in her jeans and tee-shirt and long ponytails, looking like anyone else.

It was in August, and she came with her parents to meet our family. She was scared at first. I was too. But after her mom and dad and my mom and dad had visited awhile, Becky and I started looking at each other. I couldn't believe that she was deaf. I walked across the room.

"Want to play?" I asked.

She didn't answer. She looked right at me and smiled a little. But she didn't say anything. I felt so strange. I didn't know what to do. So I just left the room.

Becky moved in the day before school opened. She came in a car with her mom and dad and five of her brothers and sisters. They all helped carry in Becky's things. I watched from the garage.

Becky didn't smile at all. Her big brother tickled her a couple of times, and her little sister gave her a licorice candy. They all hugged her and kissed her good-bye. But Becky just stood there, hardly moving.

I found a Frisbee on the woodpile and took it outside.

"Want to play?" I asked. I held the Frisbee up so she'd understand.

We played frisbee for a while. Then I found my stilts and helped Becky walk on them. She got the hang of it right away. She went all the way down the driveway and back before she fell off.

Then she looked right at me and smiled. She reached into her jacket pocket and pulled out a strong string tied into a long loop. She put the string around her hands and started flipping it every which way. She ended up with the string crossed and zigzagged in a pretty design. I'd never seen anything like it.

Then Becky took the string off and handed me the loop. She grinned and pointed at the string and at me. I wanted to try it, but I didn't know how. I shrugged my shoulders. Becky put the string on my hands and showed me what to do.

Most of the time it was really nice having Becky around. Especially on rainy days. Then we painted pictures or did gymnastics. Sometimes we made puppets or helped my dad make chocolate cake. We played the string game, too. Becky showed me a bunch of designs. Some we did together.

"It's called Cat's Cradle," my mom said when I told her about the game Becky had taught me. "It's an old, old game, and all of the designs have names."

The one thing we had trouble with was talking. Then Becky began to learn sign language in school. She learned to talk with her hands. She began to spell out words, letter by letter, and she also learned to sign whole words at a time. My mom and dad took a class to learn sign language and they taught me. That helped because then we could talk to Becky.

Becky also began learning to read lips. We looked right at her and talked in words and sign language at the same time.

Sometimes after school Becky played kickball and foursquare with me and my friends. It went okay usually, but sometimes I got mad at Becky.

When the rules to a game were hard and I couldn't explain them in signs, Becky cried and wanted to play anyway. My friends got mad then, too. "Get her out of the game," they said. "She's goofing it up."

"Go home to Mom," I signed to Becky.

"No!" she signed back. "I want to play!" She cried harder. I took her home then, or Mom heard the fight and came and got her.

Since Becky can't hear, she can't hear her own voice either. She makes loud noises sometimes. But she doesn't know she's doing it.

One day we were at the library—my dad, Becky, and I. Becky saw a man on crutches, and she was so curious she began to point and sign.

"The man is hurt?" she signed. Then she made loud squealing sounds. People all over the library stared. It didn't help to say "Shhh," because Becky didn't know she was making sounds.

My dad explained to the man, and we left. We talked about it in the car.

"There's more she wants to say," my dad said. "She feels upset that she doesn't know all the words she needs yet."

Another time Becky was angry because she couldn't make us understand something at a shopping center.

"I want to go see the—" she signed, and then she stopped. She didn't know the sign for the next word, or maybe she couldn't spell it. She cried and squealed.

"The pet shop?" my mom signed.

"NO!" Becky signed.

"The ice cream shop?" my mom asked in sign language.

"NO!" Becky signed. She cried again and wouldn't let my mom near her.

A man was watching. "Look at that bratty, spoiled kid," he said to his son. That made me mad.

"She is not bratty," I said. "She can't hear. That's all." The man's face got red and he hurried away.

Later these things didn't happen so often because Becky's signing got better and better. Besides, we got used to it too. It was just part of Becky.

One night my mom and I had an argument over my piano lessons. School had just started, so Becky was back with us. My horrible piano lessons were starting the next day. I tried and tried to tell my mom that I didn't want to play the piano. She wouldn't even discuss it, she said. I had to take lessons at least one more year. A half hour of practice a day, she said.

I didn't want to cry, but I got so mad that I couldn't help it. Then I felt someone touch my shoulder. It was Becky.

"Let's go upstairs," she signed. She put her arm over my shoulder. We went to her room and I cried awhile. It was nice to have Becky with me.

A little while after that Becky and I decided to change her bedroom back into a playroom and have my room be a bedroom for both of us. Then we had more fun together. When we had pillow fights, Mom told us to stop it. It was funny to see her yelling at us in sign language!

Becky will be with us for only one more month. It'll be summer then and she'll go home. Next fall she'll be going to a boarding school for deaf children. I felt sad when I heard about that. Dad told me just last week when Becky and I were helping him wash the car.

"Why can't she stay here and keep going to this school?" I asked.

My dad handed Becky and me the bucket of soapy water and a rag. "Her parents believe that she'll get a better education there," he explained. "But don't worry. We'll always be friends with Becky."

"But Becky's almost my sister!" I said.

That night in our room as Becky and I talked using sign language, I thought about how I'd miss her. I told her that she could come back and visit. We talked about what her new school would be like.

Then we put on our nightgowns and played with the cat. Mom came into the room.

"Time to sleep, girls," she said and signed.

We got into our beds and Mom turned out the lights. I reached for Becky's hand, like I did every night.

"Good night," I spelled with signs into
her hand. "Sleep well."

"Good night," Becky's hand spelled back.
"Good night."